MICHAEL HAGUE

Where Fairies Dance

To Maria Modugno
—M.H.

Acknowledgments

"The Fairies Dancing," by Walter de la Mare. Used by permission of The Literary Trustees of Walter de la Mare and the Society of Authors as their representative.

"Fairy Fashion," by Valerie Worth. Reprinted by permission of George W. Bahlke.

Where Fairies Dance
Copyright © 2004 by Michael Hague
Adapted from THE BOOK OF FAIRY POETRY © 2004 by Michael Hague
Manufactured in China.

Library of Congress catalog card number: 2007933136
ISBN 978-0-688-14009-0 (trade bdg.) — ISBN 978-0-06-146868-1 (lib. bdg.)

Typography by Jeanne L. Hogle
1 2 3 4 5 6 7 8 9 10
❖
First Edition

Where Fairies Dance

Selected and illustrated by

MICHAEL HAGUE

HarperCollins*Publishers*

ARTIST'S NOTE

When I was young, a long, long time ago, my family went camping in the woods. While my parents were busy making camp, I took a stroll in the forest. For a kid who grew up in the concrete and asphalt of Los Angeles, being by oneself in nature was magical. It was there that I saw a little man no bigger than my hand running across the forest floor. He wore on his head a red mushroom hat. I saw this: my word of honor.

I ran back to camp and told my father what I had seen. He shook his head and told me it was a mouse or a chipmunk. How could this be? I knew what mice and chipmunks looked like and they looked nothing like a little man with a red mushroom hat. I found my mother and told her my story. Her reply was much better. Lucky you, she said. Yes, indeed. Lucky me for I believed I had caught a glimpse of the faerie realm.

I tell this story publicly for the first time, knowing full well that many will laugh and think me daft—or worse, think I made the whole tale up. It is true. Every word. And the passing years have convinced me that what I saw that summer day long ago was not a chipmunk or a mouse but a little man wearing a red mushroom hat.

Is it really so difficult to imagine other worlds existing side by side with our own? The popular string theory suggests the existence of eleven space-time dimensions. Science continues to discover new little universes existing within our own world. From the depths of the ocean to the microcosm of plants and insects come new discoveries of wonder and amazement.

Some form of faerie exists in every culture across the globe. Could it be that the faerie realm endures within the collective subconscious of mankind? If so, perhaps we can find this world in our dreams if not discovered in the forests of our childhood.

My wish for you, dear readers, is that you someday catch a peek of this other world. In the meantime, please enjoy this faerie book and let it inspire your imagination. In the words of my mother: Lucky you!

"We are such stuff as dreams are made on, and our little
life is rounded with a sleep."
William Shakespeare, *The Tempest*

MICHAEL HAGUE

CONTENTS

The Noon Call

Hear the call!
Fays, be still!
Noon is deep
On vale and hill.
Stir no sound
The Forest round!
Let all things hush
That fly or creep,—
Tree and bush,
Air and ground!
Hear the call!
Silence keep!
One and all
Hush and sleep!

—WILLIAM ALLINGHAM

Call of the Fairies

Over hill, over dale,
Thorough bush, thorough brier,
Over park, over pale,
Thorough flood, thorough fire,
I do wander everywhere,
Swifter than the moon's sphere;
And I serve the fairy queen,
To dew her orbs upon the green.
The cowslips tall her pensioners be:
In their gold coats spots you see;
Those be rubies, fairy favours,
In those freckles live their savours:
I must go seek some dewdrops here
And hang a pearl in every cowslip's ear.
Farewell, thou lob of spirits; I'll be gone:
Our queen and all our elves come here anon.

FROM *A Midsummer Night's Dream*
—WILLIAM SHAKESPEARE

Fairies

There are fairies at the bottom of our garden!
It's not so very, very far away;
You pass the gardener's shed and you just keep straight ahead—
   I do so hope they've really come to stay.
There's a little wood, with moss in it and beetles,
   And a little stream that quietly runs through;
You wouldn't think they'd dare to come merry-making there—
      Well, they do.

There are fairies at the bottom of our garden!
   They often have a dance on summer nights;
The butterflies and bees make a lovely little breeze,
   And the rabbits stand about and hold the lights.
Did you know that they could sit upon the moonbeams
   And pick a little star to make a fan,
And dance away up there in the middle of the air?
      Well, they can.

There are fairies at the bottom of our garden!
 You cannot think how beautiful they are;
They all stand up and sing when the Fairy Queen and King
 Come gently floating down upon their car.
The King is very proud and very handsome;
 The Queen—now can you guess who that could be
(She's a little girl all day, but at night she steals away)?
 Well—it's ME!

—ROSE FYLEMAN

The Fairies Dancing

I heard along the early hills,
    Ere yet the lark was risen up,
Ere yet the dawn with firelight fills
    The night-dew of the bramble-cup,—
I heard the fairies in a ring
    Sing as they tripped a lilting round
Soft as the moon on wavering wing.
    The starlight shook as if with sound,
As if with echoing, and the stars
    Prankt their bright eyes with trembling gleams;
While red with war the gusty Mars
    Rained upon earth his ruddy beams.
He shone alone, low down the West,
    While I, behind a hawthorn-bush,
Watched on the fairies flaxen-tressed
    The fires of the morning flush.
Till, as a mist, their beauty died,
    Their singing shrill and fainter grew;
And daylight tremulous and wide
    Flooded the moorland through and through;
Till Urdon's copper weathercock
    Was reared in golden flame afar,
And dim from moonlit dreams awoke
    The towers and groves of Arroar.

—WALTER DE LA MARE

Fairy Fashion

They may take strange
Forms, but never say
They can't be seen—
Only they have a way
Of rearranging things,
Of fitting together
Cold lily-silver
Bodies and dark-netted
Dragonfly wings,

A way of using roses
For faces, dew-
Globes for eyes, and
Spider-silks for hair—
Even their clothing of
Faint moonlight is no
Disguise, but just
The common fashion
All the garden wears.

—VALERIE WORTH

Ariel's Song

Come unto these yellow sands,
And then take hands;
Curtsied when you have, and kissed
The wild waves whist,
Foot it featly here and there,
And, sweet sprites bear
The burden. Hark, hark!

FROM *The Tempest*
—WILLIAM SHAKESPEARE

Song

We, that are of purer fire,
Imitate the starry quire,
Who, in their nightly watchful spheres,
Lead in swift round the months and years.
The sounds and seas, with all their finny drove,
Now to the moon in wavering morrice move;

And on the tawny sands and shelves
Trip the pert fairies and the dapper elves,
By dimpled brook and fountain-brim,
The wood-nymphs, decked with daisies trim,
Their merry wakes and pastimes keep:
What hath night to do with sleep?

—JOHN MILTON

The Fairy Queen

Come, follow, follow me,
You, fairy elves that be;
Which circle on the greene,
Come follow Mab, your queene.
Hand in hand let's dance around,
For this place is fairy ground.

—ANONYMOUS

The Road to Fairyland

Do you seek the road to Fairyland?
     I'll tell; it's easy, quite.
Wait till a yellow moon gets up
     O'er purple seas by night,
And gilds a shining pathway
     That is sparkling diamond bright.
Then, if no evil power be nigh
     To thwart you, out of spite,
And if you know the very words
     To cast a spell of might,
You get upon a thistledown,
     And, if the breeze is right,
You sail away to Fairyland
     Along this track of light.

—ERNEST THOMPSON SETON

The Fairy Boy

A little Fairy in a tree
Wrinkled his wee face at me:
And he sang a song of joy
All about a little boy,
Who upon a winter night,
On a midnight long ago,
Had been wrapt away from sight
Of the world and all its woe:
Wrapt away,
Snapt away
To a place where children play
In the sunlight every day.
Where the winter is forbidden,
Where no child may older grow,
Where a flower is never hidden
Underneath a pall of snow;
Dancing gaily
Free from sorrow,
Under dancing summer skies,
Where no grim mysterious morrow
Ever comes to terrorise.

—MOIRA O'NEILL

Fairy Shoes

The little shoes of fairies are
So light and soft and small
That though a million pass you by
You would not hear at all.

—ANNETTE WYNNE

The Fairies Have Never a Penny to Spend

The fairies have never a penny to spend,
   They haven't a thing put by,
But theirs is the dower of bird and of flower
   And theirs are the earth and the sky.
And though you should live in a palace of gold
   Or sleep in a dried-up ditch,
You could never be poor as the fairies are,
     And never as rich.

Since ever and ever the world began
   They have danced like a ribbon of flame,
They have sung their song through the centuries long
   And yet it is never the same.
And though you be foolish or though you be wise,
   With hair of silver or gold,
You could never be young as the fairies are,
     And never as old.

—Rose Fyleman

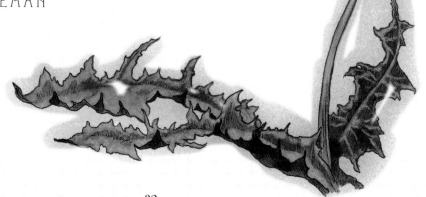

32

The Fairies' Song

We dance on hills above the wind,
And leave our footsteps there behind;
Which shall to after ages last,
When all our dancing days are past.

Sometimes we dance upon the shore,
To whistling winds and seas that roar;
Then we make the wind to blow,
And set the seas a-dancing too.

The thunder's noise is our delight,
And lightnings make us day by night;
And in the air we dance on high,
To the loud music of the sky.

About the moon we make a ring,
And falling stars we wanton fling,
Like squibs and rockets for a toy;
While what frights others is our joy.

But when we'd hunt away our cares
We boldly mount the galloping spheres;
And, riding so from east to west,
We chase each nimble zodiac beast.

Thus, giddy grown, we make our beds,
With thick, black clouds to rest our heads,
And flood the earth with our dark showers,
That did but sprinkle these our bowers.

Thus, having done with orbs and sky,
Those mighty spaces vast and high,
Then down we come and take the shapes,
Sometimes of cats, sometimes of apes.

Next, turned to mites in cheese, forsooth,
We get into some hollow tooth;
Wherein, as in a Christmas hall,
We frisk and dance, the devil and all.

Then we change our wily features
Into yet far smaller creatures,
And dance in joints of gouty toes,
To painful tunes of groans and woes.

—Anonymous